Passion's Blood

Cherif Fortin & Lynn Sanders

Genesis Press, Inc.

Passion's Blood

ISBN: 1-885478-65-8

Manufactured in Canada

First Edition

Book Design by:
Fortin & Sanders Illustrations

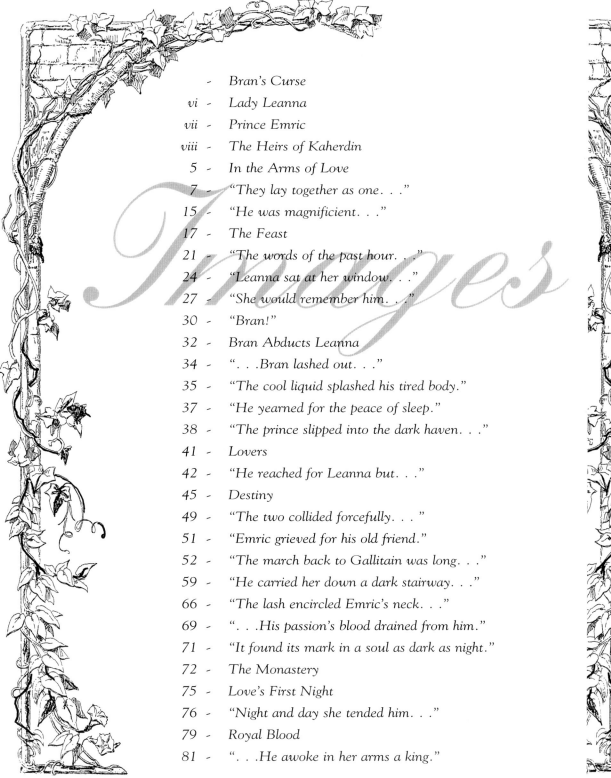

With thanks to Lynn for sharing her dream. . .

Cherif

Lady Leanna

Prince Emric

The Heirs of Kaherdin

ord Gareth brought his sword down in a mighty arc, cleaving his assailant's upraised buckler in twain and hurling him to his death from the top of the palisade. He spat a bloody oath as another of the woad-painted savages, his eyes as wild as a mad dog's, clambered over the merlon, steel gleaming menacingly from his fist.

"Fall back!" he shouted, even as he parried the dagger thrust and brought his blade down. There was the snap of bone and Gareth heaved the slumping figure back over the wall. "Fall back," he roared again. "We'll be hemmed in!"

As if in echo to his words, a thunderous crash shook the fortress as the main gates cracked. The Heldann horde raised a soul-shattering howl of triumph. With a final groan, the gates collapsed and were heaved aside by the tide of the Highland warriors. The courtyard flowed crimson as the defenders fell beneath the sheer savagery of the Heldanner's assault, who slew what came before them with steel, with primitive stone, and naked hands and teeth.

Gareth tore his gaze away from the terrible spectacle and moved along with the few of his men who still lived. As they climbed up the north tower stairs, the enemy poured over the walls behind them.

At his side a youth, blood streaming from a gash at his forehead, closed and barred the door. Others piled wood and debris to form what they knew would be but a short-term deterrent.

"Where did they come from? By God, where did they come from?" the lad babbled, eyes wide in total panic.

Gareth seized the coil of mail at the youth's neck and led him down the stone-lined corridor until he and his remaining men burst into the great hall.

"We'll make our stand here," Gareth bellowed with grim determination. His grey beard was spotted with foam, his mail awash with crimson. He wiped a bloody hand across his brow and gestured toward a group of men near the wall.

"You there, barricade the door. The rest of you, clear the center of the hall."

A dark-haired woodsman who had taken refuge in the fortress and fought as well as any of Gareth's own, wiped gore from a long hunting knife. "This is unnatural, m'lord," he gasped between heaving breaths. "The tribes this close to the Saber River do not fight in such numbers."

"They do today, by the blood of the Father," swore Gareth. Privately, he feared that some unknown force had united the hordes so that they fought with such ferocity that the keep of Gallitain was being sundered around him like kindling. "Let us pray our riders made Brimhall."

He took a quick mental count of the remaining defenders. "Damn," he murmured to himself, "just over two dozen, not enough to-"

A sudden resounding crash cut him short as the Heldanners brought their battering ram to bear against the doors of the hall. Men moved away from the ramshackle barricade of furnishings to the center of the chamber as the echo of the ram filled the air with a sound not unlike the tolling of a funeral knell. Already the boards were splitting near the edges. With gritted teeth, they awaited the inevitable, none but Lord Gareth daring to speak.

"You've done the king proud this day, lads," he said, tightening the fastenings of his shield so that it would not slip from his numbed arm. "Let us give these cursed Highlanders a reason to remember the name of Wareham." He lifted his bloodstained sword to the ready.

When at last the doors shattered and the barricade was forced aside, it was not to the roar of a slaughter-maddened mob, but to a silence infinitely more ominous. Dozens of clansmen, dripping with gore and panting with the exertion of their murderous fury, poured into the hall. Their faces bore wolfish grins and their steel glimmered like moonbeams as they surrounded the stalwart defenders of Gallitain.

From their midst strode a tall and powerful figure, clad in furs and circular plates of steel sewn to a leather jerkin. His dark hair was braided around a face as wicked to behold as the sweep of the notched axe he held in his mighty grasp. His eyes sought and found Lord Gareth and he smiled, licking his lips in some private anticipation too loathsome to contemplate.

"Kill them all," he said flatly in a voice like the grinding of heavy stones. "But leave their chieftain to me."

The horde howled and rushed in.

et's rest here a moment," Leanna called, dropping gracefully to the ground and letting her grey mare free to graze in the sweet heather. "I tire of the ride."

She laughed softly to herself for, in truth, she had another reason for stopping. Running to the edge of a glade that seemed to be fashioned of dark green velvet, she threw herself down in the billowing grass, which was woven with delicate wild flowers and dancing with butterflies. The merry burble of a brook a short distance away fell like music onto her ears.

Prince Emric smiled as he dismounted, amused by the energy his betrothed had for someone who professed to be so fatigued. Although Leanna was ahead of him, it took him only a few strides to catch up with her. He knew this was a game and he was eager to play, for Leanna's deep, passionate nature and independent spirit constantly surprised and delighted him.

Leanna's back was to him when he reached her, her red hair gleaming in the sun like wild, silken ribbons.

He fell to his knees beside her, gently touching her shoulder as she turned to face him. Pleasure surged through him as he saw that she had undone her saffron surcoat and loosed the laces of her chemise, allowing her breasts to be caressed by the warmth of the sun.

Emric slid his arms around her and buried his face in her softness. Lightly he kissed her, teasing the pretty pink buds with his lips and tongue. Then he leaned back to look at his lady, his heart filling at her perfect beauty, her delicate, creamy skin. In the past, they had always met in secret, in the shadows of the night when they had only fire-light. Today, he rejoiced that they could enjoy each other in the wild, open fields, their love lit by the pure golden sunlight.

Leanna flushed with desire as she watched his eyes drift lazily over her. Helping him with her movements, she let him push the remaining layers of cloth aside. When his hands traveled up her thighs, her hips pushed forward, seeking his body. Smiling, she pressed her palm against his heart, pleased with how it had begun to pound with desire. Eager to inflame him as she had never done before, she quickly bared his broad shoulders to the sun.

Her fingers on his skin aroused Emric and while holding her against his chest, he tossed his scarlet cape on the ground beneath them. Carefully he laid her on the silken bed and leaned over her.

Tenderly he ran his tongue along the seam of her lips again and again until she parted them to allow him entry. Only then were they joined in a deep, passionate kiss.

Gasping for breath, Leanna pulled back, thinking that her lover could extract the very life from her with his kisses. Taking his face in her hands, she combed through his long black hair with her fingers as she stared intently into his smoldering green eyes.

"I am yours, my love. . ." she sighed. Her lips pursed as a playful urge seized her anew. "You must teach me the ways of a truly sensuous woman. I want to please you like no other." Her hands traveled down his face and neck. "Guide me," she whispered.

Emric's breath quickened as her hands roamed lower. "Oh, Leanna, love." He laughed softly. "You already please me beyond measure."

Rolling onto his back, he lifted her over him, guiding her knees forward so that she straddled him. Taking her hands, he kissed her palms. Then he placed them on his belly and guided them lower and lower still.

Leanna's heart leaped with excitement as she realized that he wanted her to caress him. She had touched him before, but only fleetingly and in the heat of passion. Now he was inviting her to explore him.

Slowly, deliberately, she encircled him with her fingers, feeling his warm skin, his shape and hardness until his flesh seemed to heat beneath her touch. Bending over him, she pressed her lips to his belly. He moaned and she felt him take her head in his hands and gently push her further down. As the crisp hair brushed over her mouth, her pulse raced with adventure. Did she dare kiss him there? The thought excited her as her mouth drew closer and closer. . . .

Holding her breath, she raised her head and slid her fingers around him. Breathless with excitement, she opened her mouth and let her tongue follow the delicious contours of his shaft. She cherished this extreme and intimate connection.

Emric watched her, his eyes half-closed with passion. With a deep murmur, he pressed his tense body into the scarlet fabric beneath him, knowing that he was totally in her power.

Leanna heard Emric's moans, felt his body stretch and pulse beneath her touch and thrilled to the ecstasy she was building with her mouth and hands. She leaned back to marvel at his beauty.

Grasping the last of his control, Emric drew himself from the edge of release. Reaching up, he cupped her face and threading his fingers through her hair, brought her sweet lips to his.

"My darling, I must have you," he breathed against her mouth. "I burn for you."

He slid his hand between their bodies and found her sweet and wet, completely ready for him.

Leanna moaned as he touched her. Allowing her head to fall forward, she buried her face in his neck and submitted to his strength.

Swiftly, unable to wait any longer, Emric rolled over and fitted their bodies together. Closing his eyes, he joined them with a movement of his hips. He wanted to go slowly, but his passion spurred him on and on. Her cry sent him over the edge and he thrust into her one more time, exploding as she tightened around him.

They lay together as one, their bodies wet against the damp red silk. Even their hair tangled, completing its own mating ritual.

Finally, Leanna laughed, pushing Emric's wayward locks back from his face. "There you are," she teased. "Now I can see your handsome face."

"I need never make love again." Emric sighed. "This moment was all too perfect, my lady."

Leanna only smiled and held him close, for she knew the depth of his passions. It was good to have him home at Brimhall Castle again, and the words found their way to her lips.

"They lay together as one, their bodies wet against the damp red silk."

His dark lashes veiled the sensual fire in his eyes. He smiled and stretched like a sleepy cat in the heat of the afternoon sun.

"The date of our betrothal is rapidly approaching, Emric, dear heart," she began as she propped herself up on one elbow. "Methinks many a young lady at court will soon have cause to mourn." She traced a blade of grass over his muscular chest.

He arched a dark eyebrow. His reputation for being a rake was, he thought, quite undeserved. He did not deny the occasional liaison, but his exploits with the opposite sex were greatly exaggerated. If truth be told, since their fathers' announcement of their intention to join the houses of Kaherdin and Clairemonde by marrying their second son and only daughter, he had virtuously remained celibate. Well, he grinned, at least virtuously monogamous.

"I must profess my innocence, my lady." His mouth still curved in a roguish grin. "The idleness at court has made me victim of vicious rumors. If anyone will be in mourning, it will surely be the gallant Sir Bracchus." He traced a single finger down her neck and between her breasts. "If I am not mistaken, he holds the distinction of having been your most ardent suitor."

"Next to you," she chided. "Sir Bracchus is a dear man and it is not his fault you are so much more charming."

"And handsome," he said as his finger continued its journey over her breast.

"And handsome," Leanna agreed, her breath catching at his caress. "And courageous, witty and oh. . .so much more dreadfully conceited."

She watched him shrug his shoulders noncommittally as he laughed. Since the announcement of the intended betrothal, the last year had been a confusing time. Initially, Leanna had been furious over the helplessness of the arranged marriage, but Emric had astonished her by embracing the prospect wholeheartedly and courting her as though the union had been his own intention.

Indeed she had been flattered at the attentions of the kingdom's most eligible knight. True, his elder brother would inherit the throne, but nothing, not even a kingdom could make life with Prince Bran bearable. Emric, on the contrary, was the substance of every young girl's fantasy, possessed as he was of the most intoxicating charms, an indomitable spirit and a noble heart. She had grown to love him deeply. So why, she asked herself, did she continue to feel discomfort at the notion of a marriage with this man?

Suddenly she recalled her mother, two summers before her untimely passing, standing at Yn' Dunnall in the south of Wareham, the ancient circle of stones she had said was holy. Her mother had whispered that in her youth she and her sisters gathered there in secret to practice the Ningal, the old way, and to recite and reaffirm the oath before the Goddess.

To hold as sacred the right of will. To never bend knee to a man save as an act of volition. To never marry save in the time of one's own choosing. To never bear a child for another's pride or insistence, but from mutual desire and determination.

But these were not her beliefs, she reminded herself. She could not even recall the rest of the oath. Why should they ring true for her now? Her own mother had renounced her Druid order for a life with her father. Mutual desire and determination. . . What would she do, she asked herself, when the time finally came to speak the words, to take Emric as her husband?

Despite the delightful games she played with Emric, her trepidation mounted as the time of the betrothal grew closer, but she ignored it. She glanced at Emric, who looked as if he were about to fall asleep, but surprised her when he spoke.

"I hope you're not beginning to doubt me, my dear."

"Of course not." She smiled, concealing the pang of guilt his query aroused in her. How could she tell him? She sat up, gathered her clothing and brushed the wild grass from her hair. Then she stood and walked to her mare, which had wandered only a short way from where she had dismounted.

Emric regarded her quizzically, sensing that something had gone wrong with the mood their union had produced, but uncertain how best to put his concern into words.

"Have I disturbed you in some way, Leanna?" he asked, as he rose and donned his tunic.

She smiled reassuringly as she mounted her horse, then cast a glance over her shoulder. "Not at all. . .but those storm clouds on the horizon disturb me well enough."

Emric looked past her at the dark gray band to the west that spread up from the horizon. "We had best make for the castle or we'll be taking our chances with that weather." As he mounted, she was already urging her horse in the direction of Brimhall.

"Aye," Emric murmured to himself. "Storm clouds indeed." He spurred his steed onward to catch up.

The keep of Brimhall Castle was alive with anticipation of the Summer Feast. In the courtyard, pages busily hammered together huge tables to hold the varieties of food and drink that even now were emerging from the kitchens. Smoke wafted skyward from the many bonfires the men had laid to light the revelry long into the night. Groups of young girls were on the parapets, decorating them with all manner of gaily colored trappings. Nearby, the sounds of horns and pipes could be heard as bands of minstrels and jugglers began impromptu performances. No one chose to notice that the good Friar Corbin had yet to return from his inspection of the wine and ale stored in the cellars.

Lady Leanna watched the tumult of activity from the relative quiet of her balcony in the northernmost tower. She had returned from her ride hours ago and, to the relief of her governess Mirabel, had bathed and abandoned her riding clothes in favor of a festive gown. Mirabel had departed for the kitchens, promising trouble for any slackers and leaving Leanna to study the North Gate in the breezes of the early evening. The storm clouds had passed with only a light showering of rain and she found the ensuing coolness refreshing.

The sight of the massive stone gateway made her recall the many times Emric had ridden beneath it on campaigns to the west. Every time they had parted he had flashed his best smile for her, adding a wink, as though he knew with all certainty that he would return. And he always had returned, riding through that giant portal atop his charger, the wind tangling his long, dark hair around his handsome face, his eyes searching for her on her balcony.

Leanna's heart beat nervously as she thought of her father, who had sent her away to the relative safety of Brimhall while he defended the frontier from his holding at Gallitain. Despite the motherly attention Mirabel lavished upon her, she missed him and yearned to see him again, though she admitted conflicting emotions as she remembered how he and King Morien had reveled loudly at the idea of grandchildren. She flushed at the memory. Would she have no say even in this, the most personal of all decisions? she asked herself.

A commotion in the yard below interrupted Leanna's reverie as two men came into view and faced off. Both were hard-limbed, broad-shouldered and clad in noble finery, but the resemblance ended there. One was clean-shaven with closely cropped tawny hair and brilliant blue eyes. The other was dark, his thin beard emphasizing the cruel line of his mouth. His black hair framed a face made hard from years of strife. Leanna recognized him as none other than Prince Bran, Emric's elder brother and heir to the throne.

A group of men crowded around the two and Leanna could hear the fair man shout an accusation.

"You are ill-mannered, Your Highness," he cried with the heat of youth. "Should you not proffer an apology, I will demand satisfaction." His gloved hand went to the hilt at his side.

"Come then, Sir Owen, and satisfy your honor."

Leanna gasped at the hissing tone of Bran's reply and saw Owen hesitate to draw his sword.

"I cannot engage Your Highness in single combat," he finally said, apparently resigning himself to accept Bran's insult.

"Have no fear, Sir Knight." Bran emphasized the last word as though it were distasteful to him to speak it. Then he turned and addressed the crowd that had gathered round.

"Let no man present hold falsely against Owen that he acted against his oath as a knight in engaging in this duel of honor, be I prince or no. Unless. . ." he paused, his eyes alive with menace, his lips curled in an evil grin ". . .unless, of course, it is cowardice that binds him."

At that final affront Owen drew his blade and both men adopted a fighting stance.

The combatants began to circle one another in a slow search for an opening. Bran's blade was a thin line held low, an invitation for Owen's strike. Owen raised his weapon and thrust. As the clang of steel against steel echoed up to her balcony, Leanna watched the mortal combat in stunned horror.

Suddenly, she heard Owen cry out as one of Bran's swift parries knocked him off balance. The prince's blade whipped out, sending a dark red line across the blond knight's cheek. Owen's hand went up to his face and came away dripping with blood. With a curse, he pulled a fighting dagger from a sheath at his belt.

Leanna's spine became as ice as Bran broke into hideous laughter, unclasping his black cape and holding it loosely with his free hand. Owen drove forward savagely, cutting back and forth in wide arcs with his sword. Bran was hard-pressed, barely able to dodge his opponent's desperate strokes, but as Owen lunged forward with his dagger, Bran brought the cape up with a skillful movement and tangled the knight's weapons.

Then, spinning in a tight circle, Bran brought his blade across the back of his adversary's knee. The stroke split Owen's flesh open and sent him in a heap onto the cobblestones.

Horrified, Leanna watched as Bran circled his crippled opponent who had rolled into a tight ball of agony at his feet. As he lifted his blade for the final blow, his gaze found Leanna standing on her balcony.

She stood frozen, unable to dislodge herself from Bran's penetrating stare. Many times before he had looked upon her with naked desire in his gaze, never bothering to conceal his covetous lust. But now she saw something else in his eyes, something that frightened her more than his wanton leers ever had. It was a look of pure exhileration at the agony he had caused.

Unwittingly she knew his thoughts as if he had spoken aloud. *My adversary's pain shall redeem me in your eyes*. Horror in her heart, she gripped the railing of the balcony.

Bran sheathed his blade and smiling, extended his hand to a man at the edge of the crowd. "Bring me my whip," he said.

On a nearly unconscious level Leanna had been aware that she, too, possessed the Ningal, her mother's hereditary gift. Many times she had received impressions of other's thoughts, but they had always been unbidden and vague. Never had they been so strong.

Now, still locked in Bran's frightful stare, she understood that through her gift the eyes of the mind had opened to her his anger and hatred. She could no more detach herself from the cruel savagery of his inner being than she could turn away from his vicious eyes.

The attendant deposited a thick coil of black leather on the prince's open palm. Bran's fingers curled around the whip and then, with a flick of his wrist, it unfurled to its full length.

Leanna gasped as the whip lashed forward like a montrous snake, striking Sir Owen on the back of his legs. She covered her ears at his high-pitched scream, but could not shut herself away from the horror that was unfolding beneath her balcony. Again the whip cracked, sounding even louder, then again. . . and again.

Bran drew back for another vicious blow, but was stopped short as a mailed fist seized his wrist.

Emric's voice was furious as he yanked Bran around to face him. "No sooner do we lose one enemy, dear brother, than you must seek out a new one amongst our allies." Emric signaled a squad of men-at-arms to disperse the crowd.

In the confusion of the duel, Leanna had not seen Emric approach, but now her heart raced at the sight of her love.

"It was fair combat, Emric," Bran spat at his brother, pulling his arm free. "Sir Owen challenged me and I accepted as befits the laws of chivalry."

"Of course," said Emric, narrowing his eyes as he took a step closer. "And how does chivalry regard the torture of an unarmed man? I have ridden into many a battle with Sir Owen, of the noble house of Loriel, and I know that he is a just and brave knight. Your actions this day have cost our father a dearly loved vassal."

"The king has knights aplenty, brother, and no need for one who fought so rashly," Bran burst out. "Or perhaps you think me a liar when I say that it was he who cast the challenge?"

"If Owen yet lives, it is he I shall ask for the truth."

The brothers regarded each other for a long, dangerous moment. Then Bran smiled and took a step back.

"There were witnesses, brother. In any case, I take my leave of you. All this fighting has given me a fierce appetite." He inclined his head ever so lightly in a mocking bow. "I trust the matter is at an end." Spinning on his heels, Bran strode out of the courtyard, his retainers trailing behind him.

Emric watched his brother disappear through the inner gate, then ordered his men to attend the fallen Sir Owen. A slight motion from above caught his eye. He looked up and saw Leanna. She had pressed her hands against her breast and even from this distance he could see that she was trembling. He sent her a reassuring smile, but she only stared at him in response.

A herald's trumpet marked the official beginning of the Summer Feast. Villagers had already filtered into the castle courtyards from outside the walls. Now they milled about with the jugglers and performers, and they partook with abandon of the heaping platters of food and freely flowing ale.

Lady Leanna, still overwrought from the combat she had witnessed, waited in the great hall as the royal procession entered though the massive, iron-bound doors. King Morien, his sons at either hand, led the assemblage. Attendants scurried aside as the mighty king, known to all as the Lion of Wareham, took his place at the head table.

"Let the feast begin!" he commanded and emptied his jewel encrusted goblet as the assembled nobles cheered.

At once, the hall exploded into activity, pages bringing all manner of exotic meats, steam rising from them in fragrant clouds, from the kitchens and Leanna wondered how she would be able to eat even a bite. A servant, struggling under the weight of a huge platter, deposited a large bird, decorated with its own brilliant plumage, onto the table.

"A peacock!" exclaimed a certain Count deBracie with delight, edging forward to examine it in amazement. "King Morien has truly spared no expense this day. Such beasts roam only well beyond the sea."

But Leanna paid the count little mind. Instead she leaned against Emric, anxious to discuss the troubling feelings the Ningal had raised in her earlier.

All her life she had had episodes of intuitive knowledge, which her mother described as a gift from the Goddess, passed on through the female lineage of their family. But never had it been so clear as this afternoon when she had seen inside Prince Bran.

She yearned to hold Emric closely, but propriety demanded otherwise and she had to be satisfied with a lingering brush against his body.

"You look ravishing, my love," he whispered, smiling warmly at the sight of her.

She, too, looked at Emric with approval. He was magnificent in his dark chausses and a rich burgundy tunic, finely embroidered in gold. She wished they were alone so that she could bury her face in the dark hair that fell in thick waves around his strong shoulders. He laughed then at someone's comment and, as the sound of his mirth filled the hall, Leanna felt her own spirits lifting.

She knew it was often whispered at court that many lords deeply regretted Emric had not been born the eldest. Bran's sullen moods and cruelties alienated him from a good many of Wareham's most powerful nobles and Leanna was certain the incident with Sir Owen would only widen the rift. Even the most unaware of courtiers knew the uncertainty with which the nobles regarded the succession. But Emric would not suffer the subject to be mentioned in his presence and Leanna had never pressed him to discuss it.

"So, Leanna," began King Morien, dabbing at his chin with the edge of a silken sleeve, "how fares your noble father?"

She smiled, as grateful for the king's interest as for the respite it promised from yet another of Count deBracie's less than amusing anecdotes.

"He is well, my lord, although I have not had word from him in some time."

The king reached across Emric to pat her hand. "Take heart, child. Undoubtedly his duties in Gallitain keep him engaged. It is a severe responsibility that Gareth has undertaken in securing the hinterlands, you know."

He smiled reassuringly and Leanna warmed at this unexpected display of affection.

"Thank you, Your Majesty," she managed, wishing that she could voice her

She often worried for her father, who commanded a lonely outpost on the frontier of Wareham, where the fertile lands surrounding the Saber River had begun to attract droves of settlers. Clashes with the barely civilized tribes of the Heldann Highlands were common, but her father had insisted their lack of organization made them more of a hindrance than an actual threat.

She had barely slipped into her reverie when a sudden gasp from a nearby noblewoman roused her.

Standing at the entrance of the hall, framed by the massive, metal-bound portals, was the veteran Captain Aelfric, commander of the castle's garrison. He had entered the hall and formally saluted. His countenance was stern and there was the light of concern plain in his eyes.

"What is it, good captain?" queried the king loudly, as all the guests looked toward the man.

The soldier took a step forward. "There are heralds without to see Your Grace. They are Heldanners and they carry the banner of diplomacy."

A great clamor arose from the assemblage at the news and King Morien stood, his noble features fixed in deliberation. Then he raised his hand calling at once for silence.

"Bring them in, Aelfric, let us hear what tidings these messengers bear."

Leanna pressed close to Emric, whose apparent disquiet heightened her own. Never before had Highlanders ventured from their wilds in the region men dubbed Heldann, except to raid the farmsteads and settlements along the border. Their appearance here was distressing. She cast a glance at Bran, who seemed particularly intent on the developments.

Four men, armed with sword and round shield and clad in the peculiar banded armor and furs of the Heldann warriors, entered the hall. The stoutest held a tall spear from which depended a dark blue banner. They glared at the group of feasting nobles with something akin to disgust.

"Morien, King of Wareham!" one of them shouted, striding ahead of the rest. "We have come in the fashion of your people to bear a message from King Lorcan of

Heldann."

"King Lorccan?" asked Morien. "Why has this king not made himself known to us before?"

"I am Angvard, war-leader of Clan McQuillan, come recently under the banner of King Lorccan," said the Heldanner spokesman, "as have all the clans west and north of your borders. My lord has not had cause to acknowledge your holdings until now."

King Morien ignored the slight. "Say your message," he commanded.

"The lands you once called Gallitain now lie in ruin by Lorccan's hand and the might of his warriors," the Heldanner stated plainly.

Leanna gasped in horror, deaf to the clamor of disbelief from the assembled nobles.

"Along the river you call Saber," the barbarian continued, "your farmsteads burn and the women bewail the loss of their weakling men. The earth is red with the blood of your dead." To emphasize his point, he unfurled the standard which had hung in the hall of the fortress at Gallitain and threw it to the ground.

Prince Bran stood, his face drawn in lines of outrage, and reached for his sword, but his father stopped him, gripping his wrist. The king, too, stood in turn, narrowed eyes flashing with anger.

"So let there be war between our peoples then. Go and tell this Lor. . ."

"There is more!" shouted Angvard, heedless of his blatant arrogance before the king. "You are commanded to withdraw from your holdings west of the foothills we call Agarra, leaving those lands to be administered as Lorccan chooses. You may continue to rule the remainder of Wareham, provided you agree to pay tribute, the manner of which shall be decided by my master.

"I am further instructed to say that if you fail to obey, you will all surely die. As we swept down upon Gallitain, reaping your warriors like sheaves of ripe grain, so shall we descend on Brimhall itself and there will be none amongst you to stop us."

Prince Bran leapt up again, drawing his blade. "My lord father," he cried. "I beg

beg you, let me skin these worthless barbarians and send their hides back to their dog of a king. The only tribute they'll take from Wareham is a sword through the belly. . ."

King Morien silenced his son with an imperious gesture. "As long as I draw breath, not a single league of my kingdom will I yield to this Lorccan," he roared, his face livid with outrage. "Tell this insolent chief that if it is war he wishes, then he has found it. He will count his tribute in Wareham arrows, one for each of his cowardly followers." Raising his arm he balled his fist.

"Now go, before I lose control over these men and must watch them cut you down."

Angvard laughed harshly and spinning on his heels, clattered from the hall.

The king lowered his great lion's head to his breast. "There will be no tourneys on the morrow," he proclaimed. "We shall have real war soon enough."

The sudden din of activity in the hall drowned the sound of Leanna's grief-stricken weeping.

Emric dismissed his squires to linger a moment in his apartments. He crossed the room to the giant hearth where a dying fire sputtered and crackled. Lost in thought, he poured himself a cup of wine from a decanter that stood nearby and drank deeply, the words of the past hour still echoing in his mind.

"This Lorccan fancies that declaring his mastery over a few savage tribes will earn him the fellowship of kings," his father had said. "He shall come to curse his foolish ambition."

A general hum of approval had risen from the assembled lords as they bent over their maps, while Aelfric moved small wooden figures about the charts, plotting the movements of Wareham's troops.

"Never fear, we shall crack this impudent fool like a nut, Father," Bran cried, pounding his huge, clenched fists upon the table. "I swear to you. . ."

"The words of the past hour still echoed in his mind"

"Swear us no oaths." Emric had interrupted his brother. "This Highlander is no weakling for us to easily break and sweep aside. Forget not that he has already taken Gallitain, no mean feat for even the mightiest army."

Some knight protested, but the king silenced him. "Emric speaks truly. 'Twould be a grave mistake to underestimate him, else one day his banner may fly from Brimhall's very walls. Aelfric," he said, turning to the grizzled captain, "what say you?"

"I will not lie, Sire. We are outmanned." He cleared his throat. "We have but a few hundred here, with less than a hundred horse. Prince Bran's garrison at Karvoie has twice that number and Loriel has three hundred here." He pointed to a spot on the map. "But 'twill take days to assemble them. If we had but a few weeks to raise our levies. . ." He gestured helplessly.

"Emric," the king had turned to him, "you have fought at Gareth's side against this foe before. What make you of them?"

"When we forced the Highland clans back beyond the Saber, they were disorganized savages with naught more than bronze swords and spears who did little but raid border villages. If this Lorccan has power enough to unify the clans, they will be formidable, for they are vast in number and fight without fear of death.

"To worsen matters, the hills and forests around Gallitain are to their liking. They can sally out at their leisure to slaughter along our borders."

"But they will not be content with Gallitain," Bran said. "It was plain enough that Lorccan desires all of Wareham."

Emric nodded and a silence descended upon the council chamber as the king bent his head in thought. When he finally spoke, his voice was loud and clear.

"Aelfric, send half a dozen of your fastest men to Loriel with orders to march half his number to Gallitain and levy what he can from his vassals and peasants.

"Bran, leave a detachment at Karvoie and march the remainder to Brimhall for our protection."

He looked to Emric then and spoke, his voice tinged with deep emotion. "Now, to you, my son. Would that another be at my command, but I must ask this of you. Take Brimhall's men and ride with all haste to Gallitain. The enemy's number is great, but you must engage and detain them until reinforcements can reach you. Else we are completely unprotected."

All eyes on him, Emric bowed low, his face hard and set. "I shall not dishonor you, Father. I shall give a good accounting of Wareham courage."

King Morien nodded. "All to your tasks. Good fortune and may God speed you all."

As the assembled men had filed out of the chamber, the king had reached out and gently placed his hand upon Emric's shoulder. Nothing more was spoken between them for mere words could not contain their emotion.

Now Emric tore his gaze from the embers of the fire. His preparations were nearly complete, but his heart was heavy. He had fought often enough against the Highlanders, had seen them slake their steel in the blood of men, heard their feral howls of joy at the slaughter.

He knew that his father had no choice, for Emric was best suited to this gruesome task. But fear for those he would order into a battle that could well be suicide hung about him like a dark cloud.

The prince stormed from his chamber and traversed the long stone lined corridors of Brimhall. Soon he found himself before a stout wooden door he had seen a thousand times before but which now appeared before him as though it were the first, or the last. He cast open the heavy portal and stepped inside.

Leanna sat at her window and in the stillness of her chamber, he could hear the clatter of armed men in the courtyard below. When she turned to face him, he saw she had been weeping, and bitterly Emric recalled it had been but days ago that he had vowed to her nothing would ever separate them again. He wondered if some part of him had known he could never keep this oath.

Crossing the chamber in three great strides, he took her into his arms. Even as he crushed her to him, it seemed that his arms were already letting her go.

Leanna pressed her lips against Emric's as his hair fell across her cheeks and mingled with her hot tears.

"Leanna sat at her window. . ."

"I cannot bear it that you are leaving me, my love," she whispered. "If my father is dead, you are all I have left."

He looked down at her lovely face. "I must." Lifting his hands to wipe away her tears, he forced a smile onto his lips. "But I will come back to you, I swear it."

She shook her head and new tears slid down her face. "You swore that you would never leave me. How can I believe you now?"

"Have faith, my beloved." He took her hands and pressed them against his chest. "Listen to my heart beat and know that it beats only for you. How could I not come back to you?"

She said nothing, but only looked at him, her eyes wide and full of doubt and Emric wondered if she somehow saw the fear that his confident words had concealed.

Leanna looked at Emric. He was smiling and his words were easy and reassuring, but she felt such disquiet in her heart, for the Ningal was telling her his innermost thoughts as clearly as if he had spoken. Suddenly needing to reaffirm the reality of their love in the face of his fear and hers, she brought her hands up and gripped his hair.

"Make love to me, Emric." Her voice was urgent. "Make love to me so that I will feel your body against mine when you are gone." Her voice caught. "So that I will have something."

The ache within his soul grew as he lifted his love and carried her to the bed.

Undoing the fastenings of her robe, he quickly pushed it back and filled his hands with her soft curves. She arched up toward him and he buried his face between her fragrant breasts.

They lay quiet for a moment until he felt her shift beneath him. Despite the sadness within him, he smiled against her skin, feeling her eagerness. Lifting his head, he began to touch her.

His hands mapped her body as if he would memorize her with his fingertips.

Leanna's head thrashed back and forth on the pillow. He was touching her everywhere but where she wanted to be touched most and soon she would certainly go mad.

Emric knelt beside her, caressing her. Slowly, he let his hand slide up her thigh.

"Come to me now, my love," she whispered brokenly. "Please."

But he did not move over her, sliding instead his fingers into her hot, moist sheath. He touched her until she cried out and started pulsing around him.

Emric held her close. It took long moments for Leanna to have the strength to open her eyes.

"Now you," she whispered and reached out to press her palm against his most private place.

But Emric shook his head, he was already sitting on the edge of her bed. "No, I would remember you like this. He looked down at her fiery hair swirling around her ivory shoulders and cascading across her breasts. He marveled at her delicate lips glistening in the firelight. When I am victorious, then I will take my pleasure."

Before she could protest, he kissed her once and rose from the bed. Something in his eyes made him seem suddenly cold and more unyielding than ever she'd known. As though her very presence challenged his resolve, and without a final word, he wheeled about stepping quickly into the hall.

Back in his chamber, Emric's squires awaited to gird him with his heavy armor plates. Picking up his blade where it lay in its scabbard, he slid it with practiced ease into the leather belt at his hip. When minutes later he descended into the courtyard and swung up onto his charger, Leanna's scent still clung to his fingers.

Leanna lay in her bed and listened to the sounds below. Once she rose from her bed to go to the window, but fell back into the love-scented sheets. She would remember him as he had touched her, loved her.

When the noises of men, armor and beasts had faded, she knew that Emric was gone, perhaps forever, and she wept.

"She would remember him as he had touched her."

Sleep was long in coming to Leanna. She had lain awake for many hours, praying and weeping in silent torment, both for her father and for Emric.

She could not believe the news that her father was dead. There was no tangible proof, yet she fought against her desire to hope that he still lived. She knew that hope would only exacerbate the pain if he were truly dead. His prospects were slim at best, for if he had been captured by his enemies, there would have been demand for a ransom.

The bitter ache within her was made even more unbearable by her farewell to Emric. Despite the heartbreaking beauty of his lovemaking, she had seen into his heart and knew the truth of his mission and his chances. He had not needed to speak, for the Ningal had shown her the words that had been in his heart. . .*my love, would that fate decree a chance for us.*

She had cursed the gift that had told her what was in his mind and heart, for it was as though she were already grieving for him.

And even when she woke, she found her face wet with tears that felt as if they would never end. The fire was dead, the room dark but for a beam of moonlight that filtered through the window. Sighing, she wiped the moisture from her cheeks.

Suddenly, she shuddered, seized by the feeling that she was not alone.

Even as a cry formed on her lips, a great, meaty hand pressed against her mouth. Sharp terror gripped her as her assailant caught both her wrists in his free hand with a strength that defied her imagination.

"Quiet, my sweet."

She heard the voice as the dark figure loomed over her like a specter from a nightmare.

"I've come to claim my prize."

With a menacing chuckle he leaned back. As the moonlight illuminated his face, Leanna recognized her assailant.

"Bran!"

She kicked at him and struggled vainly to free her hands, but her efforts were as puny to Bran as if she had been a child. Finally though, her movements annoyed him, for he swore and struck her across the mouth with the back of his hand.

The blow stung and filled Leanna's mouth with the bitter taste of her own blood.

"Enough of that, my pretty," he hissed, freeing something from his belt. "Fight me again and my next blow shall be worthy of a man."

Leanna remembered the sight of Sir Owen on the ground and Bran's laughter as the blood had poured from Owen's crippled body. Recalling the horror of Bran's thoughts, she wondered how she would be able to defy him.

She fought against the filthy cloth with which he gagged her. Bran snarled, looking like a demon in the darkness of her chamber. Seizing her by the waist, he lifted her easily off the bed and onto his shoulder. As he flung her up, Leanna became aware of two immobile shadows on the floor near the door. The shapes resolved into those of guardsmen, black pools of blood spreading from them. Leanna screamed, but only muted guttural sound escaped her.

Bran strode into the dimly lit hall, his squirming bundle an easy weight on his mighty shoulders. Several of his bondsmen were in the gloom of the hall, their blades drawn.

"Come," Bran whispered hoarsely to one of them, "I have what I desire."

They made quickly for the stairs, but came short as a naked blade emerged from the darkness.

The cloak-wrapped figure of King Morien stepped before them, his sword held high at the ready. He studied the men around him and when he spoke, his voice was loud and strong.

"What have you done here, Bran?" he demanded as the prince slowly lowered Leanna to the floor. "Sleep was denied me this night and as I surveyed the ramparts, I heard a cry. Now I find this mischief?" When only silence answered him, he roared.

"Bran!"

"Answer me, boy!"

Suddenly Bran laughed in a deep, frightening rumble.

"Destiny smiles upon me this night, it seems," he said when his mirth had died down. "But what's this you've brought for me, Father? The point of your blade?" In an instant, he withdrew his own sword, though his stance remained relaxed, almost nonchalant.

Morien stood tensely, watching the crowd of armed men. Then his eye caught the pool of blood that had spread beyond the door of Leanna's chamber.

"Whom have you killed this night?" he shouted. "And you dare to draw steel against your father and your king?"

"Oh, I dare much more than that," the prince responded icily. He made a short, quick gesture toward his henchmen. "Seize him!"

As one, Bran's men-at-arms rushed forward. The first reached the figure of the king sidelong, fouling his sword arm as it rose in defense. The desperate struggle lasted but a few tense moments before Morien was overwhelmed, his steel clattering uselessly to the stone floor.

"What treachery is this, Bran?" the king asked, his composure regained. "You go too far in this. . ."

"I do as I have always done. I do as I please." Bran gripped the king's jaw roughly in his hand, staring coldly into his father's narrowed eyes. "And you would do well to change your tone. I am no longer your whelp to be spoken to thus.

"It would please you to know my designs?" Bran's tone mocked his father. "Then I shall give you this last comfort.

"I have planned this moment with the mind of the true conqueror, for I look ahead for years where others look mere days. Lorccan came to me, his men piling furs at my feet to win my favor and I knew that he could be controlled by his ambition.

"I made him king, first over his neighbors, then the whole of the Heldann Highlands. I supplied him with steel weapons and armor, schooled his men and horses. My hand guided him throughout, even as he swept out of his lands to lay flame and

slaughter on Gallitain.

"But the cursed barbarian's pride burns hotly in his breast so that he has forsworn his pledge to the contrary and issued you a formal challenge. Had the dog bided his time, you would have learned his name at the point of his blade within these very walls." Bran roared the last with rage.

"But no matter, for the end shall be the same. My army is ready to march and with the garrison gone from Brimhall, all resistance will be easily crushed. Once Lorccan has made but a memory of my dear brother, I shall send him along the coast until his hordes are too weak to oppose me. They will have served me well."

Morien shook his head sadly. "Betrayal? But why? In time, this would all have come to you."

"Would it? I have no intention of ruling as you do, Father, feebly scraping this way and that to appease those beneath me. I would have that upstart Loriel in the south and Emric courting the nobles away from me. I would inherit civil war. Better now to take by force the whole of what is rightfully mine."

The king paled in the face of his son's ambition and his gaze went to Leanna, who lay bound against the wall.

Bran smiled, reading the unspoken question in his father's eyes. "Leanna will make a fitting queen for me when I ascend the throne of Wareham. She will be my final victory."

"'Tis madness. Madness," the king repeated, but Bran grew yet more heedless as he raved.

"It is fortunate that you come to my sword now, Morien, instead of on the battlements. Without your leadership to rally your troops, my triumph is assured." He laughed again. "I bid you farewell. Know that all you have amassed in your lifetime will indeed be mine and that your beloved Emric will soon join you in death."

With a lightning-quick motion of his sword, Bran lashed out, burying his blade to the hilt in the mighty king's chest.

A strange look, a mixture of surprise and sorrow, passed over Morien's face as he crumpled slowly to the floor, Leanna's muffled screams echoing from the walls.

"Take her," ordered Bran, as he wiped the sweat from his face with the back of his hand. "We ride for Karvoie."

He stood watching as his father's lifeblood ebbed in a pool at his feet. Then, with a last shout of triumph, he made for the stairs.

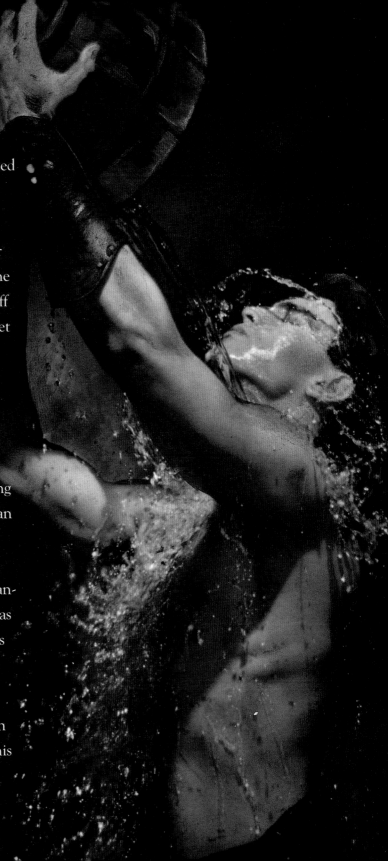

Prince Emric studied the silhouette of Castle Gallitain in the distance. The fires of the Heldann watchmen on the crenelated battlements were barely visible as heavy clouds began to obscure the midnight sky.

Having ridden at a merciless pace for days through land ravaged by fire and pillage, he and his men were exhausted. Emric shrugged off his dusty cloak and tunic, seized a nearby bucket of water, and lifted it, sending the cool liquid splashing against his tired body. But it did not soothe the fires raging within him.

He turned wearily into his tent and dropped onto his cot. Fatigued as he was, sleep still eluded him. Heavy thoughts of the morning plagued him, for he knew that they must face an opponent who not only greatly outnumbered them, but was better prepared and rested. He searched his mind over and over for some advantage, but could find none. The wisest course was to avoid open combat as long as possible unless the enemy marched for the interior.

But Emric knew they would have to fight, for the Heldanners would have no reason not to ride out at first light to crush him and his force like so many bothersome insects.

He yearned for the peace of sleep,

to leave the heavy responsibilities

behind, if only for a brief time,

and to escape into Leanna's warm

embrace. At last, the prince

slipped into the dark haven of his

dreams and there he found her. . .

"The prince slipped into the dark haven of his dreams. . . "

*L*eanna's chamber was warm in the glow of candles and smelled faintly of sweet freesia. Emric heard her moan as she fell back across her bed into the soft, deep furs. Her hair spread across the silken pillows, gleamed red in the dim light.

Reaching up, she tangled her fingers in his dark hair and guided him down to her, feeling the gentle warmth and weight of his body.

Raising himself on one arm, he lowered his head to her breast and kissed the soft roundness. Her skin was like velvet and smelled of spring flowers. Pressing his face still more firmly against her, he inhaled her fragrance and felt the arousal tighten even more in his belly. Shifting aside, he stroked his hands up the length of her smooth ivory thighs.

Slowly, he let his mouth kiss its way down her body, over her belly, and over the soft copper curls that guarded her secrets. His fingers traced her delicately, parting her silken curls to reveal her pink, wet flesh. His tongue licked the flower-like folds as his thumb and forefinger caressed her.

Then he gently spread her with his thumbs, gazing at her for a long moment before he lowered his head again and let his tongue flick wickedly.

Her cry of pleasure told him how well he could please her.

Shifting upward, his mouth suckled at her breast as his fingers entered her. Gently he moved his fingers back and forth until wanton desire was reflected in her eyes and her skin grew moist with perspiration. Her hands tangled feverishly in his hair before they slid down his back, her nails sinking into his flesh.

"Please, my love. . ." she whispered. "Do not deny me."

Her words and breathless sighs excited him beyond measure. He felt her hand reach out to find him. Freeing him, she stroked his flesh as her hungry lips sought his. He would deny her not.

The last vestiges of clothing were quickly cast aside. From the corner of his eye he caught the reflection of his crimson cloak in his armor and briefly shuddered, for it gleamed like newly shed blood.

He looked back to Leanna, who lay beneath him, her lovely body naked in the half-light of the fire. She nestled into the furs, her arms reaching for him, her legs parting for him. He lowered his body, now so hard with desire to possess her.

She gasped as he entered her. Her arms twined round his neck and she opened her mouth for his tongue and he joined their mouths as he had joined their bodies, tasting her sweetness.

He filled her and in return, the emptiness within him was also filled. He felt her move beneath him and his desire for her was so overpowering that he feared he would hurt her with his superior strength. He fought to hold himself back, yet a powerful instinct took hold of him, a need to consume her, body and soul.

She lay beneath him as delicate as a flower and he chided himself for wanting to take her with all his power. His thighs tensed as he tried to control his movements.

Then she looked up at him and her hands gripped his shoulders with surprising urgency. "Emric, my prince. . ." Her breath was ragged. "I want to feel all your strength."

He moaned. "I must have you," he gasped. His head fell back, his body tensed and arched, then he thrust into her again and again, holding nothing back. His desire for her owned him.

On the brink of release, he stopped and held her tightly against him, savoring the powerful sensation as his flesh throbbed within hers. Hungry to touch her yet more deeply, he withdrew and gently rolled Leanna onto her stomach. Then lifting her onto her knees, he knelt behind her.

Reaching forward with one muscled arm, he cupped her breast, his fingers rolling her firm nipple, sending striking sensations to her core.

Her back arched as he slowly entered her. With his free hand, he reached beneath her and his finger circled the slippery bud. He pulled back and felt her tense in anticipation of his full penetration.

He teased them both for a moment longer, then with one steel-hard motion he drove himself fully into her and heard her gasp with the strength of his thrust.

"Leanna. . .oh, Leanna." He murmured her name over and over, his mouth hot on her skin. His body set a pounding rhythm deep inside her. Both hands on her breasts, he caressed her nipples and she moaned with pleasure at the ardor of their loving.

He felt her tighten and pulse as she approached the brink of ecstasy. As he felt her climactic moment, he too exploded and then felt nothing but his own blinding release.

When the flood of sensations had receded, he opened his eyes. A motion caught his attention and he looked to the nearby pile of clothing and stained armor, which now, strangely, had grown to include broken weapons. It glowed with a reddish light and to Emric's horror, blood had begun to flow from it.

Emric's heart constricted as a hopeless terror welled up inside him. The dream had become a nightmare.

A dark figure ran into the tent, the sounds of battle mounting from without. "They're here, my lord!" the man shouted in a panic-stricken voice. "The Heldanners attack!" As he spoke the last words, he gasped and went down under a hail of arrows.

Emric clutched at his temples, unable to understand what was happening. Then the cloth of the tent was ripped away and he saw that all around him men were dying, horses screaming as they charged, weapons clanging against armor.

He reached for Leanna, but found only the hilt of a blood-stained sword.

Emric bolted awake at the sound of horsemen entering the camp and men calling his name. His dream had turned so abruptly he still felt chilled and confused. Outside it was dark and he took a moment to gather his senses.

He rose and quickly dressed before he flung aside the opening to his tent. Two riders, their armor covered with dust, dismounted from their frothing steeds and knelt before him.

"What news?" he demanded anxiously, recognizing them as men he had sent to observe Castle Gallitain.

"My lord, the enemy has left the castle and even now approaches," said the ranking warrior, pulling a grimy hand through tangled and matted grey hair.

"How many?" Emric demanded. He motioned a squire to him and taking his water flask, proffered it to the riders. They pulled long and hard at it.

"The whole garrison, my lord," the soldier spoke again. "Easily two thousand men, mostly a foot."

The gathering throng of soldiers and knights murmured at the report, each man realizing with certainty the narrow possibility of defeating so numerous an enemy.

Emric lowered his head in thought before he finally addressed his men. "Now is the time," he shouted, "to prove the worth of Wareham steel to those who would seek to enslave us." A thrilling moment of clarity flashed through him.

"Aelfric!" he called the old captain, who had insisted on being allowed to accompany the prince on his terrible mission. "This is what we will do."

He gave Aelfric his orders, then placed a hand on the shoulder of the veteran soldier. "If the fates are with us, the predawn gloom will conceal our meager numbers." Emric managed a thin smile.

The camp burst into activity and at the center of it all the prince stood, his eyes turned eastward toward the enemy and his destiny.

From the copse that hid him and his men from view, Emric watched a stream run its course like a blue ribbon down the narrow ravine. The walls of the surrounding valley were high and he understood all too well that, while this position made an ideal trap for the enemy, it could also make a tomb for his warriors. The only escape route was behind him through a range of low hills where the rest of his men now lay concealed.

He took a deep breath. He could not know if Aelfric and his troops were ready, but he knew that it was too late to change his plans.

One of the knights nearest him called softly and pointed. Emric saw the Heldanner vanguard appear out of the gloom, savages naked but for colored mud, then the main host. Two thousand strong, their dark mass formed a deadly wall bristling with spears and fury. Lorccan's army was a motley collection fused from a dozen different tribes, but they marched with a unity only their terrible purpose could lend.

The overwhelming enemy force surged forward and although doubt lay heavily within him, Emric clung to hope as his desperate plan unfolded. Silently at first, but with a growing roar of pounding hooves that sounded like faraway thunder, Aelfric's men charged from their wooded hiding place. Two hundred lancers pounded into the soft, unsuspecting flank of the Heldanner column, smashing a bloody wedge into the force.

Highlanders fell beneath the charging hooves, lance tips piercing their armor. Turning, they faced the torrent of death that had descended on them.

"Quickly," Emric shouted, signaling to sound the charge. "We must strike before Aelfric's men are cut to ribbons."

Trumpets blasted and moments later, the assembled ranks of Emric's knights began their charge. Emric spurred his destrier in a relentless gallop, pounding down the long slope toward the Heldanners as his archers loosed a whistling cloud overhead.

He lowered his lance, couching it at the ready as the enemy drew nearer. His breath came in short gasps; every nerve was alive with tension and the sound of his pulse seemed to fill his helmet with a roar. He saw the enemy's front lines going down, dissolving under the bright hail of clothyard shafts from the bowmen.

Then came a gigantic crash as the first of his knights rode headlong into the sea of flesh, sending lengths of razor sharp death into the lines. Horses filled the air with screams and men shouted their dying breaths as the charge crumpled into the wall of Heldanners.

Emric fought beside his men, discarding his now broken lance and drawing his sword.

The two Wareham forces were nearly upon each other; the ploy had been well reasoned. As Aelfric smashed the Highlanders' flank causing the main body to turn in an attempt to rid itself of the ambush, Emric's charge had fallen upon the unsuspecting foe with murderous force. A good third of the Heldann column lay bleeding or dead on the blood-soaked earth or had fled in panic into the wilds.

A Highlander ran toward Emric, howling and swinging his blade, but the prince urged his destrier forward, cutting the man down. His mount reared as he found himself beset on all sides. Blows rang against his armored thighs and clamored against his shield. Many times his blade bit into yielding flesh and Emric soon found himself covered with the blood of dying men.

All around him the Heldann host surged forward and he cursed, realizing the force of his surprise attack was now completely spent. And still he delivered blow after blow, his arm numb with the endless repetition.

Emric fought in this way for what seemed like hours, until the tide of battle surged momentarily away and he heard Aelfric's shout as the captain fought valiantly to his side. Scarlet poured from a crease in his armor near the shoulder, but his voice held triumph.

"We've cut them to the bone, my lord. God knows, 'tis more than anyone would have thought possible. But we must sound the retreat, else the Heldanners will rend us to a man."

Emric started about him and saw that Highlanders were dragging armored knights from their saddles or cutting the hocks of the horses beneath them. Their number seemed to be swelling and he understood that his men were being slaughtered.

But to flee while the battle still raged? The thought repulsed him.

"Prince Emric," old Aelfric urged. "Escape will not be at hand much longer. There is no cowardice in living to fight another day."

Emric hesitated for a moment, then nodded. "Give the order, Captain."

He sighed bitterly taking in the sight of the pitched battle. His eye was drawn to a circle of heavily armored Heldanner swordsmen, knee-deep in the cold stream nearby. The Highlanders were tightly packed around a tall black-haired giant, who struck mightily as a berserker strikes, his great axe cleaving bone and mail alike. Something in his bearing, or in the way the warriors nearby struggled to protect him, marked him.

"Lorccan!" Emric hissed, a great rage welling up within him. He would send to hell the one responsible for the death of so many even at the cost of his own life, he thought. With a yell, he spurred his mount into the thick, slashing and hewing with reckless anger.

Someone behind him shouted for him to stop, but Emric was heedless, caught in the mad, exhilarated throes of his desperate blood lust. Men fell like ripe grain around him and soon his steed splashed into the stream, scattering warriors under its iron-shod hooves. He rode to his death as though to a feast, laughing and shouting until his war horse was cut from beneath him and he careened with a mighty splash into waist-deep waters.

Emric rose with a curse, numbly aware that others were fighting with him, and smiled grimly at the sight of Lorccan a mere stone's throw away. He charged, pulling a dagger from his belt to replace his lost sword.

The Heldanner chief wheeled his great axe over his head, swinging it across in a blow that would surely have slain the prince were it not for his helmet, which was sent flying from mailed shoulders. The two collided forcefully and at that instant, the prince's knife punctured Lorccan's mail, a great crimson tide erupting over the hilt.

Emric struggled to maintain his reeling senses as the body of his adversary slumped into the cold waters.

As he passed into unconsciousness, he saw the image of a red-haired girl in a summer meadow. She was weeping and he felt very sad indeed.

od be praised, he's alive."

The voice sounded hollow and distant, and Emric could feel someone jostling him roughly.

"My lord. My lord."

Slowly he opened his eyes, a powerful ache assailing his head. An armored man he did not recognize was cradling his head and several others stood nearby.

"My prince," the man said. "We feared the barbarian king's dying blow had slain you when you slipped beneath the waters. Thank heaven you live."

Emric could hear the sounds of battle in the distance. "Are we captured then?" he queried numbly.

"Nay, my prince," the man continued, as some of the warriors laughed. "Even now the Heldann host is scattering to the winds. Their chief dead, they are making for the hills, and our stalwarts give them chase." Gently the knight lifted Emric, providing him with a view of the fleeing enemy as they fled back out of the ravine in full retreat. "The day is ours, my lord. We have beaten the horde."

"Call back our men." Emric struggled to sit up despite the throbbing pain of his wound. "We must take Castle Gallitain now that the Heldanners are routed. Have Aelfric organize the ranks." He stood shakily and realized that all eyes had grown somber. "What is it?" he demanded.

"The captain is dead, my lord. He died protecting you from the horde as you charged Lorccan's bodyguard. He had been wounded in the first charge, but gave no indication, urging us to fight on even when we thought all hope was lost." The man suddenly seemed ashamed.

Emric was stunned with the pain of the loss. "Where?" he asked, his voice hollow.

"He grieved for his old friend"

The march back to Gallitain was long and difficult.
Only the wounded were allowed to remain in the saddle. . .

He followed the glances of the men to a place on the bank of the stream. A body lay amid dozens of others, but shrouded with a cloak in a simple gesture of respect. He stumbled toward it to grieve for his old friend.

In the span of short minutes, not a single Heldann warrior remained in the valley. Those who lived sought escape on foot in confusion, blind luck guiding some toward the freedom of the hills, others toward the marshes of the Tenair River and certain doom. Bodies littered the landscape, their twisted forms jutting heavenward as though in supplication while tattered banners flapped forlornly in the breeze. Most lay dead or dying, moaning their last in the crimson glow of the setting sun.

The march back to Gallitain was long and difficult. Only the wounded were allowed to remain in the saddle, for the horses were so exhausted that Emric feared they would not survive if pressed.

By nightfall, the weary host arrived at Gallitain finding it dark and unguarded. Emric's scouts returned to say that all Heldanners had fled.

"Let the wounded be tended immediately," Emric ordered. "And send out parties to secure the keep."

It was late in the evening when men discovered Lord Gareth's battered body in the dungeon.

The prince hastened into the row of dank cells beneath the castle and ran forth to cradle the unconscious man as the chains which bound him to the rough cold stones, were pounded loose.

"Bring blankets, and water." Emric's command was sharp and urgent.

At the prince's words, Gareth's eyes opened, his trembling fingers reaching forth.

"Prince Emric!" Gareth's voice was but a sickly rattle. "And now it seems I dream even when awake." He spoke with difficulty through cracked lips that were caked with blood.

Gareth was the hero of Emric's youth, by whose side he had fought many a time. Now he lay broken and defenseless in the prince's arms, suffering as no good man should be made to do. A bitter taste rose in Emric's throat at the thought of his beloved

Leanna and her terrible grief were she to see her proud father so ravaged.

"Emric, Emric," Gareth repeated, his eyes staring dully before him. Suddenly the film seemed to drop way from his gaze and he was alert again. "You here?. . .but the savages. . ." he grew agitated.

"Do not fret," Emric whispered, unclasping his cloak and draping it over his old friend. "The price was high, but we crushed those dogs. Gallitain is again free and you are among friends."

"Gallitain free?" Gareth mimicked, his stare drifting up to the ceiling.

Emric shuddered, wondering if Gareth's mind would ever recover from his torture. A soldier handed him a water flask and Emric held it to the older man's lips.

Gently lowering Gareth's head to the floor, Emric prepared to rise. The older man follow his movements, then suddenly reached for Emric's arm.

"My prince," his voice was hoarse. "We were betrayed."

"Do not worry, Gareth," Emric reassured him, gently prying the man's fingers from his arm. "All is well."

"No," Lord Gareth insisted, grabbing Emric's arm again with surprising strength. "We were betrayed, surprised a mere fortnight after you departed for Brimhall with half the garrison. There was no siege." His fervor grew. "They slew us all, even the women and children, but left me for the torturer's arts to suffer a death unbecoming to a warrior." He drew in a long, shuddering breath. "And all by the hand of your brother."

"What say you?" Emric stared at him incredulously, sure that his pitiable condition had provoked these insane words.

Defying his crippled body, Gareth struggled up and clutched Emric's breastplate. "I have the proof of my own eyes and ears!" he burst out. "As I lay chained and under the knife, the Highlander chief vaunted his own superior virtue, mocking that one of us could deliver another to the enemy for the sake of power." His eyes were wide and full of pain.

"He brought a man I knew to be of Prince Bran's bodyguard before me and ordered him to ride to his master with the news that his plan had borne fruit. 'Twas worse torture for me to hear those words than any my body endured." He fell back exhausted, but kept his eyes locked with Emric's. "Bran brought these walls down surely as any of the Highland clans."

It was near midnight when an exhausted Prince Emric galloped into the cobble stoned bailey of Castle Brimhall. Gareth's news of Bran's betrayal had filled his heart with anxiety over the king's safety and he had ridden like a madman.

Men were shouting after him, descending from their posts and bearing torches as Emric and his escort thundered past the rising portcullis of the inner courtyard. Emric reined in hard and vaulted from the saddle as his mount slid to a halt before a growing crowd of hastily assembling watchmen.

"Is the king in his quarters?" he demanded of a nearby sergeant.

"I. . .I beg Your Highness to accompany me to the hall," the man stammered hesitantly and Emric realized that he wore the livery of the house of Loriel.

New fears rose within him and he shoved past the man, making for the great hall, forgetting in his haste even to glance at his beloved Leanna's balcony.

Within moments, he strode through the heavy oaken doors of the great hall, sending the metal-bound portals open with a crash. A group of men were there conferring around a map-laden table. The tallest of them stepped forward, his scarlet robes partially concealing the gleam of armor. Emric recognized his fine, mature features and tawny hair.

"Lord Loriel." He stepped forward. "Where is my father?"

"Prince Emric." Loriel crossed the hall and bowed before him. He stood for a long moment, steeling himself. "My prince, your father is dead." He placed an arm on Emric's shoulder. "All Wareham grieves at the loss."

"How?" managed Emric.

"The work of an assassin the very night you marched for Gallitain. None of the murderers have been found."

Numbness spread through Emric's being as the full truth of Gareth's words was now revealed. This was what he had feared, he thought, since Gareth had disclosed a traitor in their midst. He felt a bizarre sense of relief that the long wait for the truth was over.

"Murderers?" he demanded sharply. "Why do you speak as though more than one hand is responsible?"

"I suspect at least two men, my prince," Loriel replied, "for an attempt was made on Lady Leanna's life as well. Her bodyguards were found slain."

"What?" Emric felt his heart constrict. "Is she safe?"

"We believe so. She fled Brimhall to the safety of Karvoie with your brother."

"By the saints!" Emric hurled a cup from the table into the fireplace, the wine hissing as it hit the flames. He whirled away, ignoring Loriel's astonished look. "Did you see them with your own eyes, Loriel?" he demanded when he had checked his fury enough to speak.

"Nay, Your Highness." Loriel's tone was cautious. "I but arrived from the coast this very morning. Riders dispatched from Gallitain a few days ago reached me with word of the siege; they had made for Brimhall but could not break through to the interior, so decided to turn southward to my holdings. I marched north immediately, intercepting the king's messengers on the road and finding things as they are now."

"To whom did the Lady Leanna communicate her desire to flee with Prince Bran?"

"No one, my lord," said Loriel after a pause. "Prince Bran himself informed the chamberlain. 'Twould seem that she had grown faint from her ordeal. She was seen leaving the castle with your brother's men."

Emric rubbed his hands over his face. "I have grave news, Lord Loriel." His voice trembled with his fury. "Treachery most foul has undone Wareham, and her betrayor is none other than my brother." In quick, choppy words, he related what Lord Gareth had told him. "My father's murder was undoubtedly another bloody step in Bran's plan for dominion.

"Lady Leanna despised him," he continued, pausing as a wave of grief poured over him. "Never would she have gone willingly with him."

"What would you have us do?"

"We cannot wait until the rest of your garrison arrives from the coast," Emric said firmly. "My brother does not know that you are here and I suspect that he will try to attack Brimhall, thinking it undefended. Emric strode to where Loriel stood. "We shall take the battle to him. Take what men you have and march toward Karvoie. I venture you will encounter Bran's army soon enough."

"We ride together, my prince?"

"Nay." Emric shook his head. "I shall take a dozen of our swiftest riders on a different mission." His dark brows drew together. "I have seen into my brother's black heart and he will deliver himself into my waiting hands." With those enigmatic words, he turned away to gaze into the fiercely blazing fire.

"The crown is now yours by right, my lord. It may not be the fate you would have chosen and the manner in which the crown has come to you is grievous, but you are king, and Wareham is well served by it." Turning, Loriel strode from the hall to begin preparations, leaving Emric alone with the echo of his words.

The dark spires of Bran's castle loomed in the night. Built into a cliff face at the foot of imposing northern mountains, it had been raised over the crumbling remains of a fortress built by conquerors forgotten in the long history of Wareham. Its bastions had withstood many sieges, and judging by the daunting sight of it, Leanna imagined it could withstand a thousand more. Around the walls, the campfires of Bran's army burned in the night.

Leanna, bound and gagged, had made the journey here in a carriage with the loathsome Bran. Through a crack in the curtains she spied the sickly forests which surrounded Karvoie. Disease, she recalled, had once decimated the north of Wareham long years ago and it seemed the land had never fully recovered. What people she saw resembled cadavers. Peasants, eyes hollow and dull with famine, knelt by the roadside, more in fear than tribute. It seemed to her as though she had entered the realm of the dead.

When the carriage came to rest, Bran's hands gripped her shoulders. "Welcome to your new home," he laughed as he easily scooped her up in his powerful arms. His step was light, even cheerful, as he carried her into the fortress.

Within the courtyard Leanna beheld grim faced men, armed and attending a variety of tasks. Some sharpened weapons amidst others who stacked wagons to over filling with supplies. A vast host was readying, she surmised, to march for war.

He carried her down a dark stairway to the dungeons, and entering a remote cell, dropped her unceremoniously onto a bed of damp, dirty straw. Faint threads of light filtered though holes in the ceiling and moisture ran in rivulets down the stone walls. The indescribable stench threatened to overcome her as Bran roughly unbound the ropes which held her wrists.

"I hope you find these accommodations pleasant, my lady. They are as lavish as we can afford one of your stature here in Karvoie," he bent in a mocking bow. "Soon you will again enjoy the splendor of Brimhall. . ." he paused ". . .as my queen." His thin mouth curved in a lecherous smile.

"I am not ignorant of the fact that you think me a monster. That matters little." He shrugged. "Think on this, my lady," he leaned down toward her.

"Your father is not dead, but Lorccan's prisoner. He will remain so as long as suits my fancy. Those savage Highlanders have treated him most barbarously." He shook his head in mock pity. "When I am king, I could have him brought to Brimhall, if you do your part. You will accept me as you never accepted my brother. I demand not just your submission, my lady, but sincere desire."

"He carried her down a dark stairway to the dungeons. . ."

Leanna shrank back against the wall and Bran took her waist.

"Your pretty prince is dead by now and soon all of Wareham will be mine. . .as you will, my lady."

He turned and left the cell, slamming the door with a powerful clang that in Leanna's ears echoed like the sounding of a crypt-lid.

The days passed like a nightmare. The damp foulness of the cell weakened Leanna, as a rattling cough that issued from her chest sapped what remained of her strength. What food Bran allowed her was less than meager, and at first she had guarded the stale bread and brackish water from the rats that shared her captivity.

She knew that Emric would fight with courage and she clung to the idea that he still lived, but she understood all too well that his situation was desperate. As desperate as her chances of escape, for even if she could manage to flee the castle, she could never evade the whole of Bran's army outside the walls.

As weakened in spirit as she was in body, she took to throwing her food to the rodents, believing she would rather die than further endure this agony. Starvation was a slow death, but infinitely preferable to Bran's hated embrace.

She fell into despair, sobbing until it seemed her tears were spent. Then, like a ray of morning sunlight, reason filtered through the dark of her anguish. She thought again of Emric and remembered his bravery and strength. He would expect the same from her, she concluded. He would wish her to live and to avenge the evil Bran had done.

Leanna resolved to be strong. She would be cunning. Duplicity and guile would be her shields.

Leanna awoke one morning to a thunderstorm, rain draining in thin streams from cracks in the ceiling. She crawled, shivering into a corner where a measure of dryness remained when the door swung open noisily and Bran stepped into the cell.

Lifting her roughly to her feet, he laughed. "How fares your fiery temper today, my lady?"

Only a pleading, submissive gaze greeted him and he smiled. "This is most unexpected," as he lifted her chin with his forefinger, "and delightful."

Leaning forward, he kissed her and when she offered no resistance, he crushed her to him in a greedy embrace.

When he stepped back, his eyes glowing with lust, Leanna shuddered at the evidence of his blatant arousal.

"I am well pleased to see that you are as intelligent as you are beautiful. I did not expect you to see the logic of my offer so soon." He twisted his hand in her hair and pulled her to him.

Praying for the strength to bear what was to come, Leanna did not fight him as he kissed her mouth and throat. She forced herself to lift her hand to caress his face, then faltered, doubting her ability to maintain this terrible charade.

Bran swept her up and placed her on the crude, wooden table that stood in the middle of the cell. His breath already uneven with passion, he seized her breast in a rough caress, tearing at her clothes.

Leanna closed her eyes, fearing that her glance would betray her revulsion. Bran forced her legs open and thrust his still covered manhood against her. He pinched her nipples and she cried out with the sudden pain. She heard him make an approving sound and knew that he had taken her cry for one of pleasure.

Leanna resisted the urge to fight him. Desperately her mind searched for a haven where she could flee from the impending rape. Emric's image rose to her mind and she clung to it as her last hope.

She recalled how he would seek her out in her chamber while the castle slept. She remembered how she had waited for the sound of her door opening. Sometimes he would stand at her bedside for long minutes, just looking at her.

"*What are you gazing at, my prince?*" she had asked once.

"*I am drinking in your beauty, Leanna, so that it will always be with me.*"

"*Is it enough for you simply to behold?*" she had teased him. *Staring into his eyes, she slowly pushed away the blanket from her body until she lay naked to his gaze. "It is not enough for me.*"

Inflamed by her words, her half shy, half brazen action, he had torn off his clothes and pressed his aroused body against hers in shared passion, with mutual longing.

His hands caressed her and when his fingers slid between her thighs, he found her ready. He quickly joined their bodies. . .then stilled.

Wanting more, she had moaned, "Please, Emric. . ."

Suddenly a fierce slap across her face brought her back from the dream where she had escaped. Her eyes flew open and she saw that Bran's face was contorted with fury.

"You called for Emric," he spat.

"N. . .no," Leanna stammered. "I am yours. . ."

"I warned you," he shouted and hit her again. "You will be mine without all pretense, else your father will suffer for it."

He stepped back from her, his arousal gone, and Leanna closed her eyes as her relief fought against a sense of regret at her carelessness.

"Do not think for one moment, Leanna, that you cannot be made to suffer as well," he snarled.

Turning, he opened the cell door and called out to a servant. "Ready her, we march for Brimhall in one hour."

eanna huddled, shivering against the frigid night air. Vainly, she pulled at the chains that bound her to the stout central pole of Bran's pavilion.

In silence she had suffered the indignity of a day's march slung across a horse's rump, a punishment Bran had decreed for her indiscretion. Every bone in her body ached from the ordeal.

The whole of the prince's army had marched long after sundown, driven by Bran's eagerness to attain Brimhall. When darkness made travel too treacherous for horse and wagon, it was with near petulance that he had ordered his men to make camp.

Leanna had been grateful; her trepidation and fear for all of Wareham had mounted with each passing mile. She tried her chains again.

Slowly she became aware of shouting and the sounds of frantic men outside the pavilion. Leanna was momentarily blinded by torchlight that seemed to explode into the tent.

"What is it?" she asked, recognizing Bran behind the firelight, his face panic stricken. "What has happened?"

"Loriel is attacking!" Bran shouted. He thrust his torch in a nearby brazier.

Leanna reeled at the news, her heart beating swiftly with fresh hope. Hiding her feelings, she watched Bran rage about the tent.

A man, clad only in an undertunic and hose but bearing a sword and shield, ran into the tent.

"My lord, Loriel's outriders have breached our camp," he gasped. "Our men are taken by surprise. Lest we can muster them, all will be lost."

"Return to your post!" Bran bellowed, his eyes wild. "Organize the ranks. I shall lead us to victory against this feeble rabble. Now go!"

"You are undone, Bran." Unable to contain the joy that swelled within her, Leanna rose onto her knees. "If Loriel attacks you, it can only mean that all of Wareham's lords are prepared to rise against you." Sensing his fear, she continued, her voice ever louder. "No one can help you now, not even your Heldann allies."

"You dare defy me?" he screamed, unfastening the chains that bound her so roughly that his grip threatened to snap the delicate bones of her wrists.

Leanna bit her lip so that she would not cry out with pain.

"I will yet defeat this dog Loriel." Bran's frenzy mounted. "He can slaughter this army to a man. It is lost to me already, fit only as a diversion while I return to the safety of Karvoie. I will levy another army, and muster aid from Lorccan's quarter. . . no, this is but a mere delay of the inevitable." His mouth curved in a cruel smile, "I will yet rule Wareham."

He grasped Leanna by the wrist and pulled her after him. "When the enemy takes this pavilion, you and I will be well out of reach." He laughed harshly. "And I shall have set my feet on the road to victory."

They galloped toward Karvoie, Leanna seated unceremoniously before Bran in the saddle of his giant black stallion. Escorted by six heavily armed, evil-countenanced henchmen, they rode at such a breakneck speed that she could not understand how he could hold her so fast and yet control his steed.

The sun had barely begun to show beyond an abandoned monastery on a nearby hilltop when they thundered into a thickly wooded area. Leanna started as she heard the distinctive sound of arrows slicing through the air behind her.

As Bran reined in his mount and wheeled it around, she saw that several of their escort had fallen from their saddles, crimson-shafted arrows protruding from them at all angles.

Suddenly, as if by some enchantment, men appeared from the thicket on either side of the road.

Leanna shook her head in disbelief as she saw Emric stride to stand in the center of the road. A dozen men, their crossbows at the ready, swarmed around him. He held his naked blade in his hand, his mouth curved in a cool smile.

"'Tis a misfortune the Heldanners failed to end your bothersome life, brother." Bran's tone was thick with contempt.

Leanna began to struggle against Bran's hold and he fought to control his steed. Emric took a step forward as the rest of Bran's guard lowered their weapons in surrender.

"You are the basest of cowards, Bran," he said with disdain. "I knew that you would flee to Karvoie if Loriel challenged your advance." His smile widened. "There is no escape for you now. Release Leanna and join your men."

Bran, seeing no alternative, lowered Leanna slowly to the ground. She rushed into Emric's arms.

An exaltation the likes of which she had never known filled her as he embraced her. She gripped him tightly, needing to assure herself that he was real and not some specter who had come to cruelly taunt her. All that she had suffered in the last days broke past her restraint and she began to weep uncontrollably. Not even Emric's gentle kisses could stem her tears.

"Now you will bring me to justice, I presume." Bran's eyes were hard and menacing as he looked at his brother.

"That is a privilege you do not deserve," Emric said icily. "You cannot know how many have died and suffered by your hand. . .and our father. . ." he choked back a wave of emotion. "To what avail, Brother?"

"How sweetly your display touches me, Emric." Bran inclined his head, smiling with perservse humor. "I did what was necessary to further my rightful cause. Do you think I did not see you scheming for the throne? That I did not see Loriel's rivalry?" He laughed harshly. "Did you believe I would simply allow you the succession?"

"You are mad," Emric whispered, shaking his head. "Dismount."

Bran complied, for the crossbows leveled at him offered no recourse.

"Now draw your blade." He pushed Leanna away into the protective arms of one of his men.

"What?" Leanna broke free and gripped his shoulder.

"He must die, Leanna, here and now, and by my hand."

"No," Leanna pleaded, clutching at him desperately. "No, not now that we have been reunited. I thought you dead, but my prayers have been answered." The words tumbled from her lips. "Do not place yourself in danger again, I beg you."

"I love you with all my heart and soul, Leanna." Emric touched her cheek.

"But I cannot allow my brother to live a moment longer without atoning for the evil he has wrought." Gently he pushed her away.

As he turned to face Bran, one of his men rushed up to him. "My prince, you cannot. . ."

"I must," Emric said firmly. "Do not intervene." He swept his gaze over his men. "My honor will be satisfied only if I am victorious in single combat." He waited until each member of his escort signaled their acknowledgement, then shifted back to face his rival.

"Let us cross steel, my brother."

Bran tore his sword free with a snarl and leaped toward Emric. His blade flashed like the play of lightning, feinting first toward the legs, then slashing upward. Blue sparks shimmered as blow upon blow fell on Emric's blade, forcing him back away from the escort.

Leanna watched in horror as the two men fought in grim silence, grunting from the fury of their strokes. Terror flashed through her as Bran's blade ripped across Emric's thigh. Blood mingled with sweat, but the two men fought on as the sound of steel against steel seemed to fuel their ferocity.

Emric pressed his brother with a series of powerful lunges, barely pulling his sword back in time to parry. The men locked blades for a tense moment, then Bran twisted his wrist in an expert motion, smashing the hilt of his weapon against Emric's unprotected temple.

His senses still weakened by the wound he had received at the hands of King Lorccan, the prince reeled as the blow connected. His numbed hands released the blade and he fell, valiantly struggling against unconsciousness.

Tearing at the fastening of the whip laced to his belt, Bran was upon him within the span of a breath. The lash encircled Emric's neck in a fatal embrace and Bran tightened it relentlessly.

"This is my vengeance, dear brother," Bran hissed in Emric's ear. "You were a fool to let me live. I will yet be king and Leanna will be my consort."

Emric fought the darkness that threatened to descend upon him. His lungs burned as panic rose within him, stealing the last of his breath, and his pulse pounded thickly in his temples. He would die at Bran's hand, just like their father, then Leanna would be at Bran's mercy. How she would scream with the knowledge that her Prince had failed and Bran, swollen with pride at his vengeance, would mount her to assure his complete victory.

A powerful tide surged through Emric, giving his limbs new strength, filling his lungs. Rage at the rememberance of his father's death, fury at the thought of his Leanna in Bran's filthy hands exploded within him and propelled him to his feet. He could not let his brother's insanity destroy all that he loved.

Emric thrust his head backward, feeling the snap of bone as it connected with Bran's nose. The whip was cast loose and Emric's body heaved uncontrollably to find air at last.

Struggling to his feet he beheld Bran on the ground, blood streaming from his face. He stepped back and stumbled over the hilt of his fallen blade.

Bran sensing the opportunity, lunged forth, scooping his sword from the ground. The two collided in a thunderous crash, tumbling in a mass.

Pulling his blade free, Emric rolled to his knees and with a forceful yell, raised the sword and sent it down. It found its mark in a soul as dark as night.

Bran's body crumpled, breath leaving his dying frame in a slow hiss.

Emric fell back weakly and Leanna rushed to her beloved, cradling his head to her breast, tears of relief coursing down her cheeks.

"Emric, my love," she whispered, stroking her hand down his face, watching as the anger and strain that had marked his features in battle slowly receded. "My love. . ." Her worried gaze traced his wounds, following a streak of crimson to a rent in the mail at his side. "You are hurt!"

Sinister ribbons of crimson wound their way to the ground, as his passion's blood drained from him. Leanna stared at the gleam of steel in Bran's lifeless grasp.

". . .his passion's blood drained from him."

"It found its mark in a soul as dark as night."

She had not seen when he had drawn the knife nor when it had taken its grizzly toll.

She shuddered as fear closed her throat. Grasping Emric's limp hand, she tried to steady herself, but a knot formed in her stomach. His skin was pale, his breath already so shallow that she bent to his chest to reassure herself he still lived.

Emric felt Leanna's touch and struggled to rise, to speak. . .at least to open his eyes, but he could not. The glory of victory was supplanted by the ruin of defeat as Emric realized poison had coated his brother's vile blade.

The Prince's men-at-arms swarmed around them and Leanna directed that they carry him to the cloister they had ridden past earlier. She feared that the move might kill him, but she knew they could not stay here at the mercy of the elements.

The men built a makeshift litter by lashing together spears and brought him to the nearby ruins of the ancient monastery. Most of the roof had crumbled, but shelter could be found in the far section of the wall that had remained intact.

They laid Emric as gently as possible on the blankets Leanna prepared, yet the movement produced an unintentioned wrench to the wound and he moaned, grasping violently at the air as if fighting an unseen foe.

Leanna touched his face, gazing into his distant, clouded eyes and he quieted. He whispered her name and then his eyes flickered and closed.

She pressed his hands against her heart as she studied his face, wondering if she would ever see the raging thunder in those magical green eyes again. Would she ever drown in them as she had done so many times in the past? Her heart pounding with fear, she knelt down to him.

"Don't leave me, Emric. Don't leave me now." She repeated the words over and over as if they alone might keep him alive.

But she knew that they would not and so she rose, pushing her hair away from her face.

"Build a fire," she commanded. "We must keep the prince warm. And bring water that I may clean his wound." She wished for Mirabel and her medicine pouch, but knew that she would have to rely on her instincts alone.

An examination of the injury revealed but a shallow stab, where the poignard had pierced the mail, but the cut was already swollen and discolored. With a sinking heart, she realized there must have been a poison upon the blade.

Carefully, she washed and dressed the area, but could do no more than hold him as his body struggled and tossed in its effort to escape the relentless pain. She wiped him down with a damp cloth to cool his raging fever.

"You will not die," she whispered to him. "I will not let you die."

The sun set slowly through the age-worn arches, where stained glass had once presided. As moonlight rose, Emric's magnificent body finally quieted. Despite the warmth of a crackling fire, the night grew cold and Leanna lay down beside Emric to warm him with her body.

Dawn came and then another day, and she kept her vigil over Emric, fearing at each moment for his life. When night fell again, the moon glistened with a sickly pallor and his only movement was the occasional flicker of his dark eyelashes.

Vainly, Leanna tried to cool him. Again and again, she brought a cup of water to his lips, but he did not drink of it as the fever drained his remaining strength.

His body, usually so sensual, was now diminished by the wantonness of the poison within him. The dark wound above his hip had angry patterns of scarlet tracing across his belly and groin. He groaned with some horrific nightmare.

"Do you remember love, the first time you came to me?" she whispered so that only he could hear her. "How we pledged our love and wed our spirits that moment you loved me for the first time?"

He lay silent in her arms, but she continued with the recounting of their first loving.

"You loosened the blue ribbons that held my chemise and slipped it from my shoulders, looking at me as though you were afraid to touch me." She smiled at the memory. "But I looked into your eyes and knew that I could trust you with my body. . .with my soul. Remember my love?

"I kissed your fingertips and placed your hand against my breast. I felt you shudder as you touched my skin and my heart beat so wildly I thought it would take flight.

"Our clothing dropped away as if by magic and you drew me against you. Your skin was so warm as you lifted me and put me on the bed. Gently, you spread my hair over the pillow. Twas like firelit silk, you said.

"You touched me everywhere before your fingers entered my secret place. My breath caught as a wealth of new sensations rose within me, yet I felt safe. I asked if there would be pain and you said, yes, but only for a moment. As you moved your finger within me, your thumb brushed lightly over the bud at my entrance. It was then that I began to yearn for the moment of pain, for that moment would bring you to me and make us one.

"Night and day she tended him,
sure that she was his last and only connection to this world."

"You were careful, my love, and gentle. I was eager, spreading my thighs for you, moving my hips in anticipation, but you entered me so slowly I felt I would go mad. When you cupped my body and thrust into me fully for the first time, I cried out, suddenly afraid. I had never experienced a man's passion before. You stilled within me until I drew you deeper inside me and slowly we began to move with the same rhythm, our bodies alive with pleasure. As I felt that first peak of passion, you cried out as you poured your seed into me."

Startled, Leanna snapped from her reverie as one of the men approached and set down a bowl of steaming broth beside her.

"You have not eaten in days, my lady. 'Twill do the prince no service if you fall ill as well," the squire's concern was plain in his youthful eyes.

She thanked him and ate a bit, but Emric's body seemed to heat still more with fever and she set the bowl aside.

Night and day she tended him, sure that she was his last and only connection to this world.

A terrible storm rose the evening of the fifth day. The fever raged so that Leanna bathed Emric's body almost continually. The men had withdrawn to a corner of the chamber and spoke grimly among themselves. The rider they had sent to seek help had not returned and their expressions showed they had lost hope, but Leanna refused to succumb to despair.

During the night, exhaustion overcame her, though she rallied against it, and sleep took her. Her body went limp and her hand slipped from his, breaking the life bond.

Through the haze of dreams, Leanna saw Emric. A shadow swooped down around him and she heard what seemed to be the fluttering of wings.

"No, do not hurt him," she screamed in terror. *"Who are you? What do you seek of us?"*

A hawk-like creature descended, growing as it did so to a near human form. Slowly, the unearthly figure turned and Leanna gasped as she recognized the face of Ursanne, her mother. A calm smile played on her lips and she was as beautiful as Leanna remembered.

"Oh, mother." Tears rushed to Leanna's eyes as they embraced, the weariness and pain of these last days flowing from her. "How I have missed you."

Some part of her understood that she was dreaming, but the clarity of these images was so powerful she was struck with awe.

"And I you, Maya." Her mother gently touched Leanna's cheek.

Leanna stared. She had ceased to remember the name by which her mother called her as a child.

Ursanne looked at Emric, who lay near them on a pallet. "Who is this man?"

"Emric, the king," Leanna paused ". . .and my betrothed."

"And do you love him?" Ursanne asked with a gentle concern.

"Yes, mother, above all else." Leanna heard the desperate tone in her own voice and wondered at it.

"Then why is it you hesitate?"

"I. . .I do not understand," Leanna stammered.

"Child, give me your hand." Her mother's voice echoed in the void around them. "You have the power. . .as you have always had it, for it was yours even before your birth.

"I swear to uphold the law of this order," Ursanne began to speak the ancient vow of Druid priestesses, which she had recited so often during Leanna's childhood. "That womankind shall not be deemed unworthy in the eyes of the world. That I shall pass on these teachings to the daughters of my house. To hold as sacred the right of will. To never bend knee to a man save as an act of volition. To never marry save in the time of one's own choosing. To never bear a child for another's pride or insistence, but from mutual desire and determination."

Leanna shivered as her mother completed the nearly forgotten oath.

"To hold above all else the right to love freely and compassionately for one's own sake."

As the words rang in her mind over and over again, she realized Ursanne had spoken without vocalizing, and had used the Ningal to communicate as she had done years ago in their private moments together.

"Go to him, my child. Make of this union what you will, if that is what you wish."

"It is." Leanna uttered, a sense of faith and confidence flooding within her. Slowly, her mother's figure assumed an ever more transparent, ethereal quality until it disappeared. "Mother?" she cried. "Please wait. . .I cannot see you. . .where are you?"

From the void she heard Ursanne's voice calling her name softly.

"Lady Leanna?"

One of the men-at-arms shook her awake gently. Leanna opened her eyes dispelling misty recollections of the past night's dreams.

"The prince, my lady." The man spoke with difficulty, his bearded face lined with grief. "He has during the night. . ."

Leanna's heart lurched and she turned toward Emric, reaching out to touch his pale cheek. Instead of the fever that had burned his skin, he now felt so very cold.

"No!" she screamed, scrambling to her knees.

She pressed her ear to Emric's lips, then to his heart, listening for any sign of life, but finding none. It was a nightmare from which there would be no awakening and she prayed to God that it would end.

Placing her hands on his chest, she bade his heart to begin beating again. There had always been reservation within her toward Emric, despite the love that she had borne him, for he had been forced into her life by the will of other men. Only now that he lay dead in her arms did she realize how pure was her love for him, no matter what had brought them together.

"No," she cried again, grief welling up from inside her. "You cannot die. You must live!"

Suddenly, she thought to hear a breath escape his lips. Thinking she had imagined it, she stared down at Emric. Her mother's words came unbidden to her mind, echoes of her dream. *You have the power.*

A wave of serenity swept over her. Leanna placed her hand on Emric's wound. She let her love of him flow unrestrained for the first time. A sensation of heat and strength infused her as the Ningal grew from within her mind, filling her with an all consuming light. A mystical awareness of the world around her grew and she directed it toward Emric.

The magic she wrought rushed through him and a sound, half cry, half gasp issued from his lips. His chest rose fully for the first time in days, his lungs filling with cool, sweet air, at last. . .his green eyes opened, and he whispered her name.

Tears of joy streamed down Leanna's face as she leaned down to Emric, covering his mouth with hers.

Gently, Emric returned her kiss and she knew that all would be well at last.

He had fallen in battle a prince. . .he awoke in Leanna's arms a king.